Withdrawn

Frosty

the Snowman

Frosty
the Snowman

By Steve Nelson & Jack Rollins

illustrated by Brad Davies

ODYSSEY BOOKS

Published in 2009 by Odyssey Books, a division of The Ciletti Publishing Group, Inc.
463 Main Street, Suite 200, Longmont, Colorado 80501.

ISBN 978-0-9768655-6-8

To readers of all ages
who delight
in the magic of winter,
the beauty of snowflakes,
and the story of one
beloved snowman.

Frosty
the snowman
was a jolly happy soul,
with
a corncob pipe
and a button nose
and two eyes
made out of coal.

Frosty

the snowman

is a fairy tale, they say.

He was made of snow

but the children know how he came

to life one day.

There must have

been some

magic

in that old silk hat

they found.

For when they placed it on his head,

he began to dance around.

O, Frosty the snowman was alive as he could be. And the children say he could laugh and play just the same as you and me.

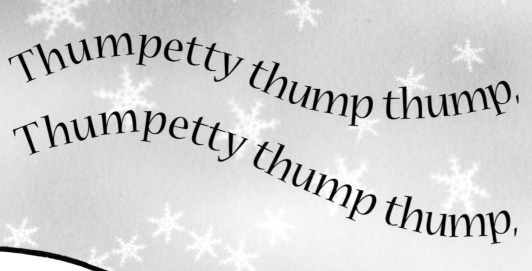

Thumpetty thump thump,
Thumpetty thump thump,

look at Frosty go!

Thumpetty thump, thump

Thumpetty thump thump,

Over the hills of snow!

Frosty
the snowman
knew the sun was
hot that day.

So he said, "Let's run and we'll have some fun now before I melt away."

Down to the village
with a broomstick in
his hand, running here
and there all around
the square saying,

He led them down the streets of town, right to the traffic cop. And he only paused a moment when he heard him holler "STOP"!

For Frosty the snowman
had to hurry
on his
way,

But he waved
good-bye, saying,
"Don't you cry,
I'll be back again
someday."

Thumpetty
thump
thump,

Thumpetty
thump
thump,

Look at Frosty go!

Thumpetty
thump
thump,

Thumpetty
thump
thump,

Over the
hills of
snow!